Barbie Fairytopia™

W9-BNS-300

Forever Fairytopia

Cover design by Diane Choi
Illustrated by Atelier Philippe Harchy

A GOLDEN BOOK • NEW YORK

Published in the United States by Golden Books, an imprint of Random House Children's Books, a division of Random House, Inc., 1745 Broadway, New York, NY 10019, and in Canada by Random House of Canada Limited, Toronto. Golden Books, A Golden Book, and the G colophon are registered trademarks of Random House, Inc. Originally published by Golden Books in slightly different form as three separate works: *Welcome to Fairytopia* in 2005, *Journey to Mermaidia* in 2006, and *Fairy Dance* in 2007.
ISBN: 978-0-375-84717-2   www.goldenbooks.com   www.randomhouse.com/kids   www.barbie.com
MANUFACTURED IN MALAYSIA   10 9 8 7 6 5 4 3 2 1

Fairytopia is a magical land where fairies and butterflies dance around rainbows.

Elina lives in the Magic Meadow with all her fairy friends. She's like all the other fairies in Fairytopia, except she doesn't have wings!

Elina wishes she could fly like her friends. They have so much fun twirling and soaring through the sky.

Some of the naughty pixies in the Magic Meadow tease Elina because she doesn't have wings.

But Elina's friend Dandelion likes Elina just the way she is!

Elina and Dandelion have a favorite game—racing through the Magic Meadow. Dandelion flies through the sky, and Elina glides through the flowers.

Help Elina find the path that will take her to Peony, her flower home.

FINISH

START

START

FINISH

Answer:

Peony is happy to see her friend and welcomes her home.

Elina's home is very cozy!

Fairies and Friends!

Look up, down, and forward to find
the names of Elina's friends.

Dandelion • Peony • Bibble • Butterfly • Sprites

```
R H C S H E W B U S R H H
L D F E N H V E S H Y H A
T W E T H T E K E U K E H
H B G I S D T R T V S J T
U H E R C B Y R E H L A N
O F S P L P H A Q T B M B
C U B S N R E H O P G T I
R P S C H I H S H E M T B
J H D A N D E L I O N H B
L T H S K M H O E N O P L
P H Y E M H T R S Y H G E
L Y T A H T N P X H L W H
B U T T E R F L Y H M H U
```

Answer:

© Mattel

© Mattel

Elina and Dandelion set out on an adventure to visit Fairy Town.

Elina meets a new friend!
Use the code to find out who it is.

= U

= R

= A

= Z

_ _ _ _ _

Azura and Elina have some sweet nectar and fairy cakes.

Azura gives Elina her crystal necklace to keep safe.
The necklace holds Azura's fairy powers.

Elina looks for her friend Dahlia.

Dahlia welcomes Elina!

The evil fairy Laverna wants Elina's necklace so she can take Azura's fairy powers, but Elina is brave and keeps it safe.

Elina has earned her wings by keeping Fairytopia safe from Laverna!

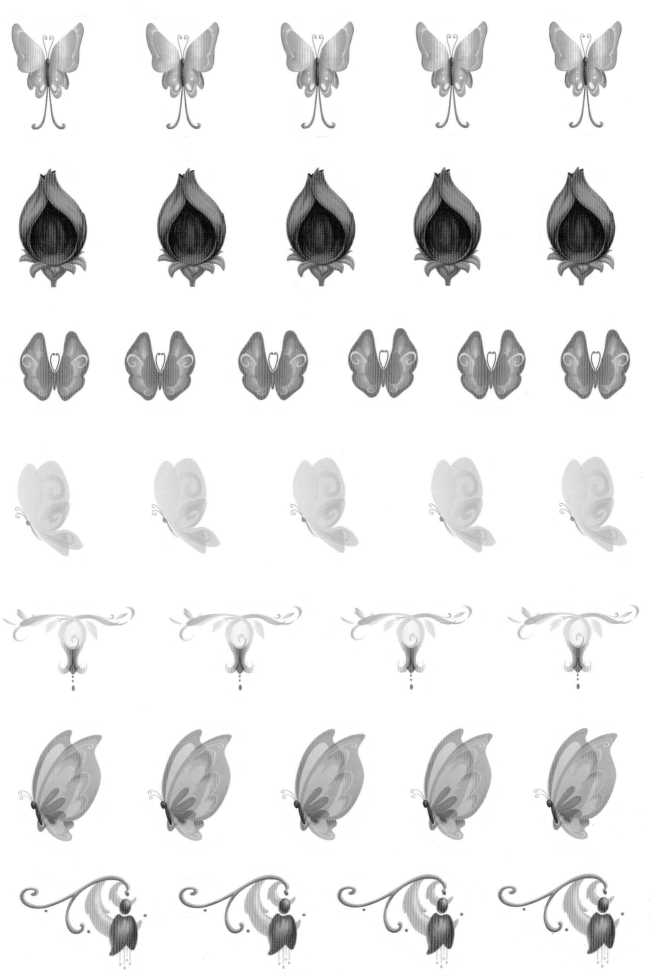

Barbie™

Fairytopia™

Now Elina can fly through Fairytopia with her friends.

Elina wonders if the other fairies only like her for her new wings.

Elina meets Nori,

Elina f

Delphine the snail tells Elina that to find Nalu, she and Nori must make a journey and work together along the way.

Use the stickers on this page to decorate your notebook or diary.

© Mattel

Nori swims by herself into the Depths of Despair and gets
caught in some plants.

Elina is not strong enough to swim down with her wings, so to save Nori, she wishes on her pearls to trade her wings for a tail.

Once Elina frees Nori, they find the Mirror of the Mist.

The mirror shows Elina and Nori where Nalu is being held.

For their bravery in the Depths of Despair, Elina and Nori magically receive the Crest of Courage marks on their arms.

Next they must cross a path filled with dangerous geysers.

At the end of the path are bushes filled with magical berries. One kind of berry, which reveals your true self, looks like the Immunity Berry! Elina takes one.

Elina and Nori find Nalu at the end of a cave.

Bibble gets Max to look away while Elina switches the berries. Now Elina has the real Immunity Berry and Max has the false one.

Oh, no! Elina's pearls have all turned white!
Now she'll be a mermaid forever!

Nori has an idea. Elina should eat the magical berry that reveals her true self.

Elina eats the berry and reveals her true self—a fairy with spectacular wings!

Meanwhile, Laverna has eaten the false Immunity Berry and has turned into *her* true self—a toad!

Elina's fairy friends are dazzled by her new wings, but mostly they are just happy that she has made it home safe and sound.

Use the stickers on this page to make a scrapbook.
You can put pictures inside each of the frames!

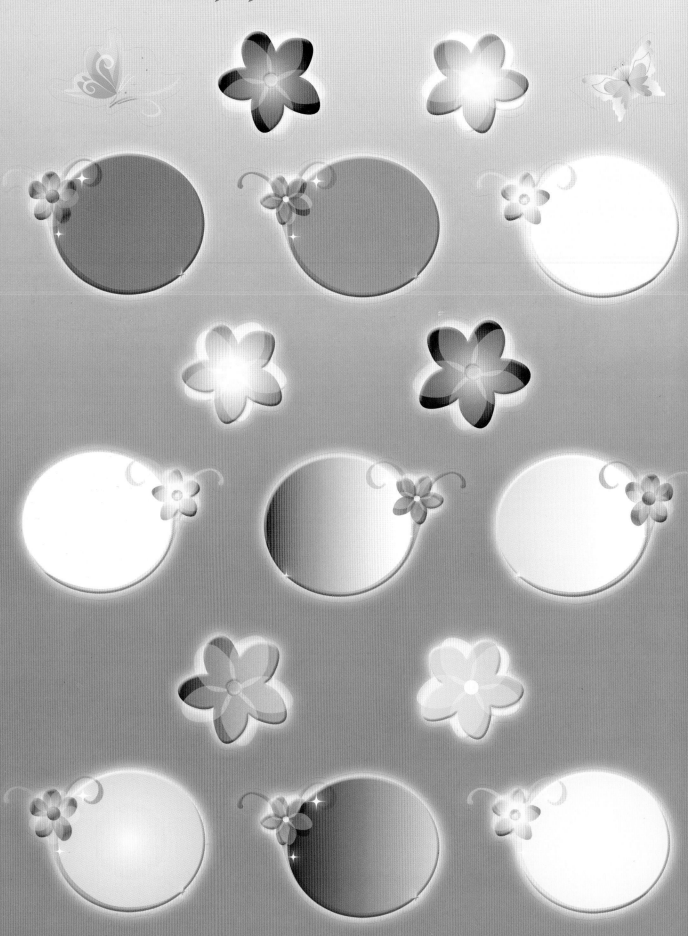

Use the stickers on this page to make a scrapbook.
You can put pictures inside each of the frames!

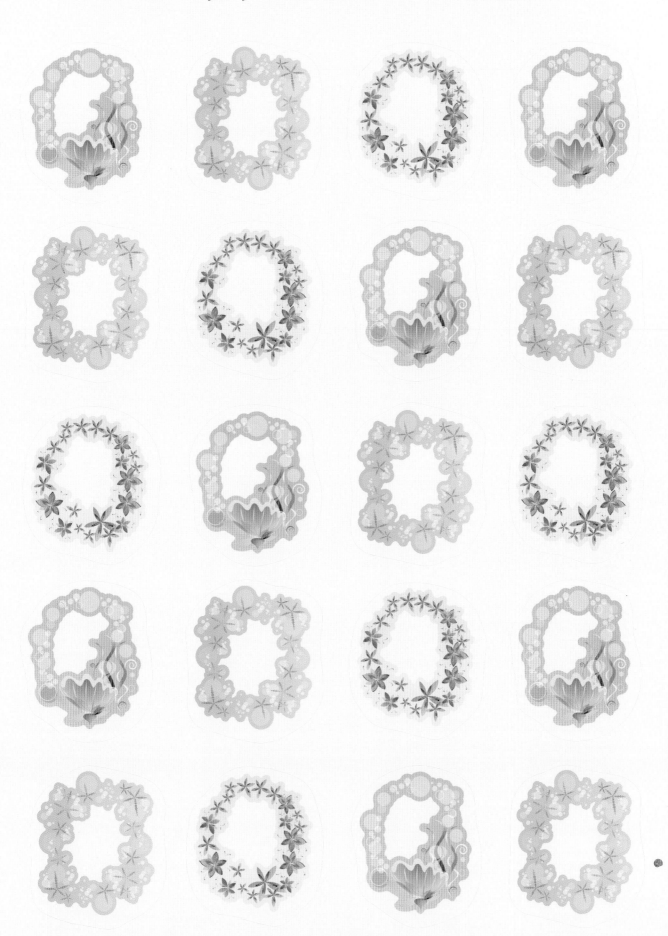

One day, Elina gets a visit from Azura.

Azura asks Elina to be her apprentice and learn the Flight of Spring, an important dance that brings spring back to Fairytopia every year.

Elina is very excited!

On her way to the Crystal Palace to learn the Flight of Spring, Elina meets Linden, another apprentice.

At the Crystal Palace, Elina meets some other students.

One fairy in particular, Sunburst, doesn't like Elina at all.

But Elina soon meets Glee, and the two become friends.

On their first day of classes, Azura explains how the Flight of Spring is performed.

Use these stickers to add frames and borders to the coloring book pages!

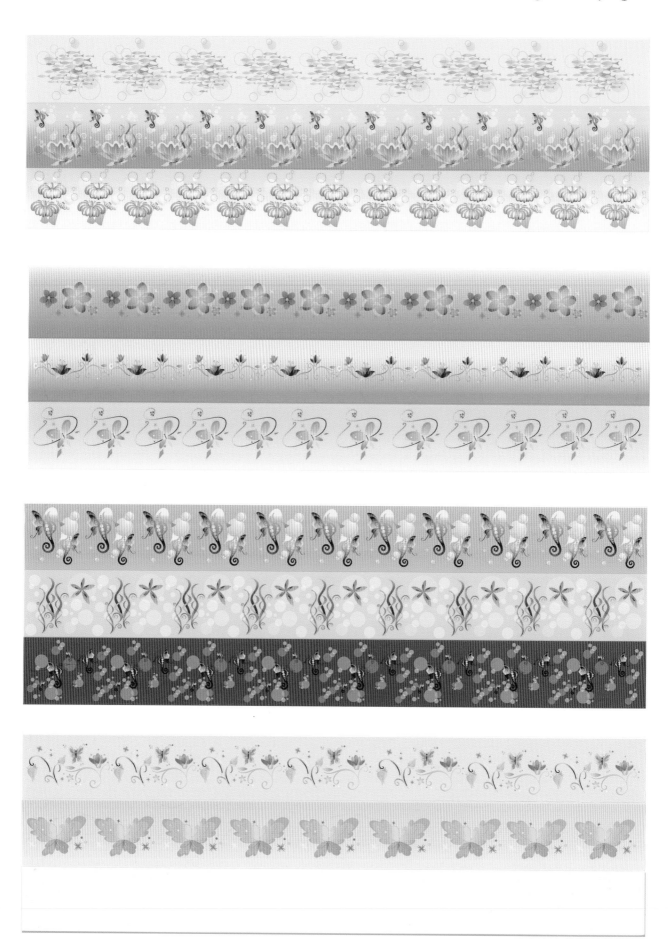

Use the stickers on this page to make a scrapbook.

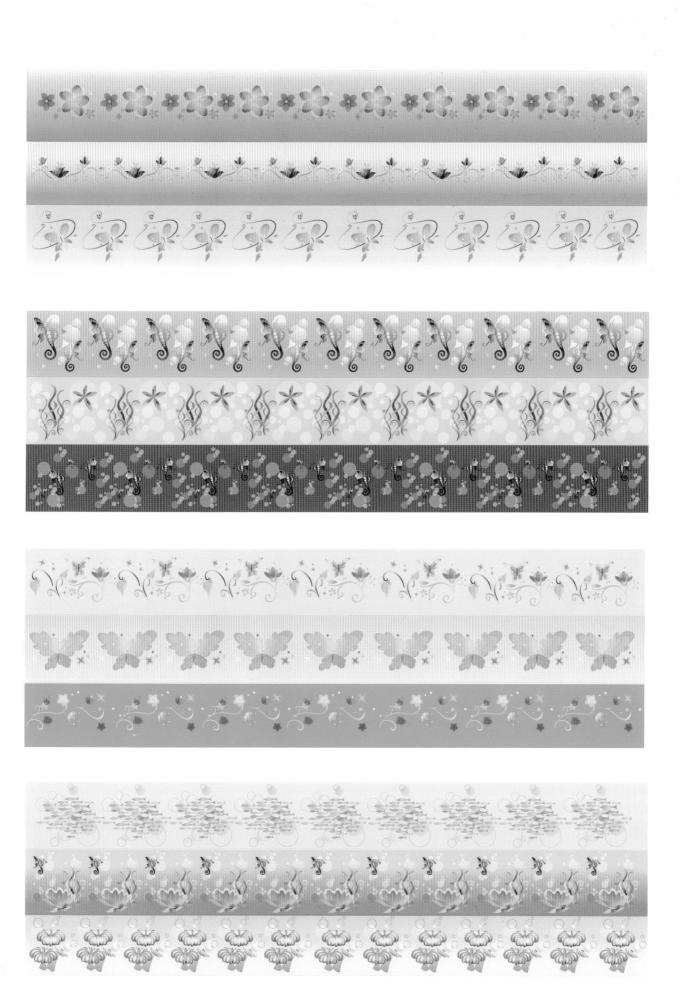

Elina does a wonderful flance (a combination of flight and dance) in flance class.

In light-throwing class, the students learn how to create objects with light. Sunburst is a natural!

Meanwhile, Laverna, in her toad form, decides she will trick Elina into turning her back into her human form. She tells Elina she is just a poor cursed toad, and Elina, trying to help, accidentally releases her!

Laverna traps Sunburst underwater and changes herself to look like Sunburst!

Finally, the time comes to perform the Flight of Spring!

Suddenly, Elina realizes that Sunburst is actually Laverna!

Elina rushes to find the real Sunburst.

Laverna changes back into her human form, and the fairies all stand together against her. Laverna is defeated!

With the stickers below, you can create all kinds of borders
and frames to decorate your coloring pages! Add the smaller stickers
to the larger ones to create your own designs.

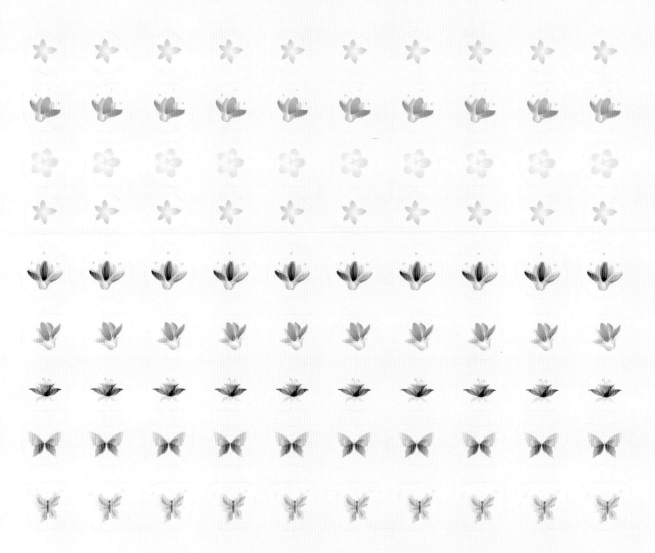

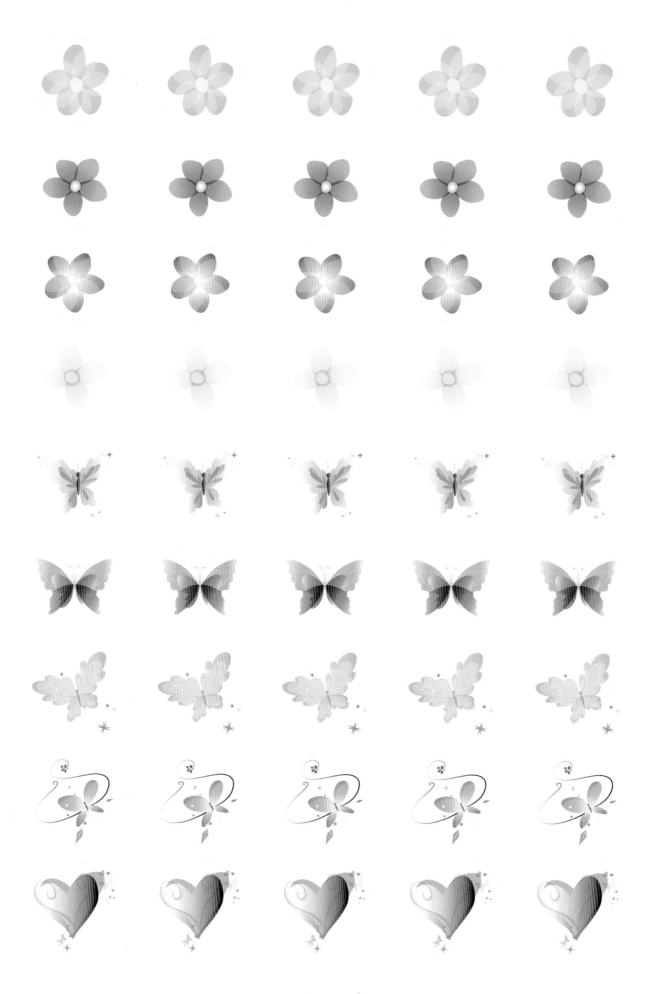

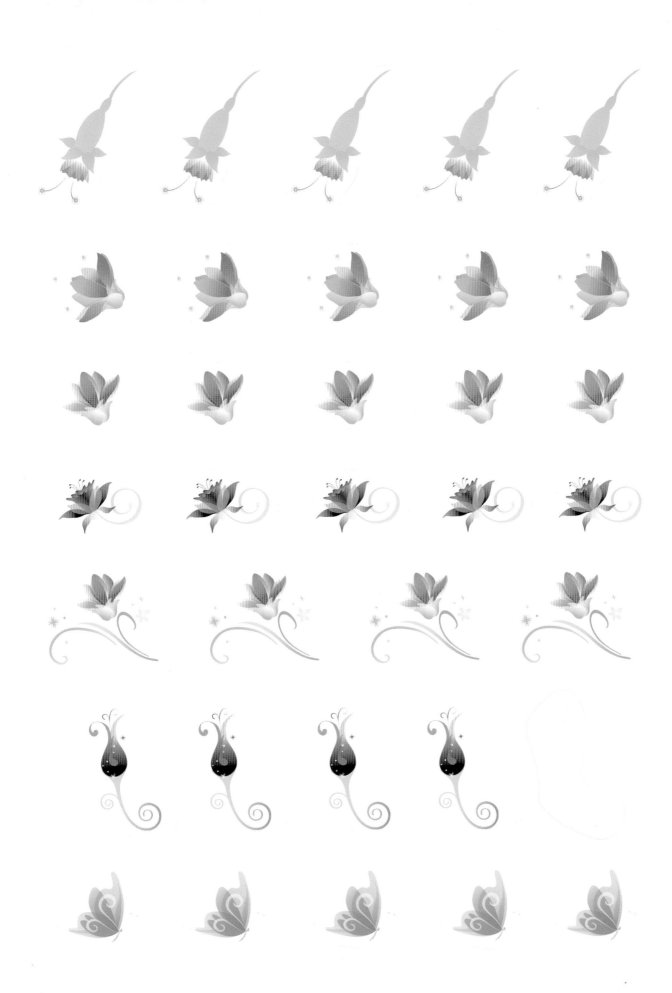

Sunburst, Elina, and the rest of the fairies quickly finish the Flight of Spring.

The Flight of Spring worked! Spring has come to Fairytopia for another year.